Slow BURN

TRACIE DOUGLAS

To Christie

They weren't lying when they said a sister will always be the best friend you can have. Your belief in me never lets me down. Thank you for being my biggest fan.

One

BEN

The clock on my dashboard tells me I'm ten minutes early as I pull into the parking lot of one of Chicago's public libraries. I reach for the hardcover suspense thriller in the seat next to me and check my hair in the rearview mirror before getting out of my truck.

My teenage daughters, Kinsley and Katie, have been here since early this morning. Their high school internship started a few weeks ago after school let out for the summer. It's a good program, keeping the girls busy and out of their mother's hair.

I didn't object to the idea of the internship, even when I knew I would have to drive an extra half an hour to pick them up on the days they spent with me. I didn't mind it because it gave me the opportunity to see *her* again.

The sexy librarian I haven't been able to get out of my head, not since the day I first laid eyes on her. It was a few months back. Since my company specializes in working on historical buildings, the city hired us to oversee some minor modernizations.

She was sitting at the main desk, the last stop on my walkthrough with the city planner and my foreman. She looked up from her book, gave us a shy smile, and answered all our questions with a delicateness I've never seen before. Her soft voice was like music to my ears; the more she spoke, the more I wanted to listen. I found myself entranced by her, soaking up every detail of the beautiful creature in front of me.

I cross the threshold, push open the door of the building, and spot her right away. She's sitting in the same place I saw her all those weeks ago. Taking a second to catch my breath, I remember the book in my hand, and then I slowly approach the desk. She looks up at me, and her eyes light up with recognition.

Mine.

Where did that come from?

I push the thought away, trying not to focus on the way my body has come alive at the sight of her. It's always like this, and I suffer for hours after leaving her.

"Good afternoon, Ben," she says, closing her book and granting me her undivided attention. When she smiles up at me, I feel it in my cock. I shift, moving closer to the desk, trying to hide my body's reaction to her. All I can think about is how much I want to make her smile like that every day, right before I bury my cock inside of her.

"Hello, Cami." I nod, giving her a smile back, fighting the primal urge to lean over and kiss her senseless. Instead, I lift my book and place it on the counter. "Thought I'd return this, since I'm done reading it."

"Great. Tell me, what'd you think of it?"

"It was pretty good. Thanks for the recommendation." When I picked the girls up last week, I asked her for a book recommendation, mostly to have a reason to speak with her.

"I have a little confession to make." Her face grows serious as she leans closer and lowers her voice. "I haven't read it, but in my defense, I've been told it's a great read."

"I see." I smile down at her. Her confession isn't surprising; she doesn't come across as the Dean Koontz type. Especially after I found myself tearing through the pages, trying to find some insight into who she is, only to come up short. "Mind if I confess something, too?"

She nods at me with curious eyes.

"I already knew that." She frowns, tilting her head to the side, trying to figure out how I knew she hadn't read the book. "I've never seen you read anything not written by Austen or Brontë, in fact, this one I've seen three times now."

She looks down at the book in front of her and places a gentle hand on top of it—*Pride and Prejudice*. I have a feeling it's her favorite, which would explain why I've seen her with it more often than any other book.

"You're very observant," she says in a low her voice and peeks up at me from beneath her thick, dark lashes.

"When it comes to you, I am," I confess, but the

sound of my daughter screeching from across the room keeps me from saying anything else.

Cursing inwardly, I turn around and spot both my daughters headed this way.

"Dad." My oldest, Kinsley, stops in front of me with a smile. I'm instantly suspicious. She doesn't smile, at least not at me, not since she discovered boys and makeup.

Cami reaches out, and our fingers brush as she takes the book from my hand. The sensation sends a shiver throughout my body. I look back at her, wondering if she felt it, too, but she's already resorted back to librarian mode, and the warmth I saw in her eyes has been replaced with professionalism. My heart aches a little, not ready for our time together to end.

"Dad," Kinsley calls again, this time gently grabbing my arm. "Can I drive home today?"

"Hi, Kins, how are you?" I ask, trying to hold back my annoyance, cursing myself for not getting here sooner. Something happened today, something between us, and I can't explain it. All I know is, I want more of it.

"Dad, please, can I drive?" She bounces from one foot to another, ignoring me.

"Don't let her," Katie speaks finally, irritation written all over her face.

"Hey, what's your problem?" Kinsley turns and faces her younger sister, her face flushed with annoyance.

"You almost got me killed this morning. That's my problem."

"Enough." My voice transforms into stern father mode, and both girls quiet down. "Now is not the time.

Kins, I'm driving you and your sister home today. You need to get better with your mother's car before you get behind the wheel of my truck. Now, please, wait outside for me."

Both girls grumble all the way out of the building, but I ignore them, quickly turning back to Cami with an apologetic smile.

"Sorry about that," I say, but she holds up a gentle hand and stops me. She smiles and lets the warmth seep back into her eyes.

"Don't worry about it. Sisters argue. I get it. I have an older sister. Don't worry, they'll outgrow it." She laughs lightly. "One day, they'll be best friends."

"I hope you're right." I exhale loudly, half chuckling, half groaning, then Katie peeks her head back in and wails at me.

"Daaaaaaaaaaad! Kins pinched me."

I roll my eyes and lift my hand, silencing Katie's complaint. Cami's shoulders shake with laughter over the situation.

"Goodbye, Cami," I sigh before turning away to follow my girls. Next time I pick them up, I 'm going to be here extra early.

As we walk to the truck, Kinsley's eyes are glued to her phone, but Katie's watch me with curiosity.

"I like her, Dad," she says softly, moving to walk next to me.

"You should like her, Katie; she's a nice lady," I

reply. Katie's always been the shy one of my daughters, so her telling me she likes someone is a big deal for her, but I don't think too much about it.

"No, Dad, I like her... for you."

Her words almost cause me to falter my next step, but I manage to hide my surprise.

"I don't know what you're talking about."

"You like her," she explains, watching as Kins throws her backpack into the front seat. She frowns but doesn't say anything to stop her, even though it's Katie's turn to sit up front. "She likes you, too."

"Katie..." I stop and turn toward her, wondering.

"You shouldn't be alone."

"Katie—"

"I mean, it's okay when Kins and I are with you, but when we're not... I worry about you." She tucks a stray strand of dark hair behind her ear. "Mom's happy with Bill. You should be happy, too."

"I'm happy," I tell her, not believing the words any more than she does.

"You don't have to pretend with me." She shakes her head before hefting her backpack higher onto her shoulder and walking past me to the truck. "Just think about it, Dad. And so you know, Kins feels the same way I do."

I take a breath to steady the pounding of my heart, and I watch as she climbs into the backseat without looking back. Hearing my daughter, knowing her concerns, I can't help wondering if she's right.

This is the last thing I expected to come from this day.

Two

CAMI

The plan was to stop by the butcher shop this morning, but I hit the snooze button on my phone a few times too many. I guess that's what happens when you spend the night tossing and turning, dreaming of the many different cuts of "meat" available on the menu, but all their faces wind up looking like Ben.

As I park my car outside The Meat Market after work, I can't stop thinking about Ben Miller and the way he looked in those jeans, walking away from me yet again this afternoon. The man is superhero hot, but it's more than that. Something about him calls to me. He's charming with a boyish smirk that would melt any woman's panties. He takes care of the people around him, like his crew, always ensuring they have what they need before heading home for the night. Most of all, he makes me comfortable.

The first time I laid eyes on him, he was walking the building with the city planner, going over the blueprints. The moment our eyes met, I melted into his dark chocolate depths. The air crackled with each step he took, intensifying the closer he came to me. When they finally stopped at my desk to ask a few questions, I found myself rambling on just to keep him near.

Never has a man evoked the emotions he has in me. The more he comes around, the easier it is for me. He came around often during his project, making up reasons to talk to me, and I found myself looking for him on the days I knew he'd be in. There were a few occasions I thought he might ask me out, but he never did.

Turning my head, I shake off my sudden disappointment over Ben and bring my attention back to the quaint building next to me. I open the car door and step out onto the street. Then I lift a hand to make sure my hair is in place before I make my way inside the building, pushing Ben out of my thoughts completely.

If he were interested, he would have made a move by now, but he hasn't, I tell myself while taking in the atmosphere around me.

The first thing I notice is the change in temperature, but then I see that no one is behind the counter. A small silver bell glints at me from the counter, and I walk over and press down on the button, alerting whatever staff is around to my presence.

"Be out in just a minute," a male voice calls from a doorway behind the counter. "Feel free to take a look around."

I shift from foot to foot because my nerves are

starting to kick in, making me second-guess my decision to do this.

What in the hell are you thinking, Camilla? I chastise myself, but before I can turn and flee, a man emerges from the doorway. A man who would make any warm-blooded woman stop and look twice.

"Hi," he greets me with a dazzling white smile, and for a moment, I'm struck dumb by the Adonis he is. "How can I help you?"

I clear my throat to speak, but words don't come easy. He smirks, clearly aware of the effect he's having on me.

Woman up, Camilla!

"Is Jason here?" I manage in a cracked voice, but my hands begin to shake as my nerves ramp up.

"I'm Jason," he says, tilting his head to study me. I take a hesitant step forward and a deep breath.

"Hi, Jason." A flush heats my cheeks. *Why does Jason have to be so gorgeous?* But to be honest, he isn't my type, and he isn't Ben. I cringe. *Shit, don't think about Ben right now!*

"Are you okay?" His brow crinkles, and his eyes fall on my hands clasped tightly together in front of me. I keep twisting my fingers almost painfully. I take a deep breath and push through, refusing to let my sudden attack of nerves control me.

"Yes," I respond, releasing my hands in the process. "I'd like to place an order."

"Sure." He eyes me carefully before pulling out an order slip from the register. "What can I get you?"

"I'd like to order some meat?" I reply with a small

chuckle, trying to be clever about the whole thing, but instead, I feel like a total dork.

"Okay, would you like to order a single helping or for a group?"

"Single. Wait, you do groups?"

"Sure," he answers, but the way his brow furrows, it's almost like he isn't sure how to answer my question. "Large orders require a minimum month's notification."

"I don't want a group order. I just want something pleasing." I relax a little, no longer feeling as ridiculous but still nervous enough I once again clasp my hands in front of me and begin twisting my fingers.

"What kind of meat would you like?"

"I'm not sure. Do you have a menu, or like a catalogue?"

"For meat?"

"Yes, I'd like to know what you offer."

He tilts his head, his curiosity written all over his face, making me feel like I've lost my mind. I stare back at him, blinking once and then twice, but he says nothing.

"Did I say something wrong?" I ask, suddenly aware of how weird the conversation is becoming.

"No, but I have a feeling we're talking about two different things." He places the order form down onto the counter and leans forward. His eyes narrow on my face, like he's trying to figure me out. "You're not here for a traditional slab of steak, are you?"

"No. I'm looking for something untraditional," I answer, feeling a little braver. His eyebrows lift, and he chuckles, clearly entertained by me.

"Are you a referral?" he asks, and just like that, whatever worries or concerns I had about Miranda making all of this up are gone.

"I overheard some coworkers talking about it yesterday."

"Eavesdropping on a private conversation?" He crosses his arms before smirking at me. My insides respond as he looks me up and down.

"Yes, er, no. Maybe."

"And you wanted to see if they were telling the truth." I nod and swallow the lump forming in my throat. He eyes me carefully, assessing the legitimacy of my curiosity. "You're serious about an order, then?"

"Now that I know this is real, yes, I'm serious about placing an order."

"What's your name?" he asks, focusing on my face.

"Camilla Babcock."

Something flares deep within his eyes when he hears my name, almost like he's heard it before.

"You work at the library?" he asks, and I find myself speechless. *How does he know where I work?*

"Yes, how did you—"

"Camilla, I know exactly what to order for you." He smiles at me, his eyes holding a secret. "Will you trust me to set you up with one of my guys?"

I close my eyes and take a breath. "I don't know."

"You came here today to take a chance. So, take it. Trust me, I won't steer you wrong." He finishes with a wink, and I can't help feeling like he's telling me the truth.

"Okay," I agree, shaking my head.

"Be ready Friday night at seven. Your date will pick you up then."

"It's that easy? How do you know what I want from him?"

"First, you need to give me your address and a credit card. Second, yes, it is this easy. And finally, whatever does or doesn't happen is between you and your date." He hands me a piece of paper, and I write down the name of a restaurant. He eyeballs it. "You want to meet up at this restaurant?"

"If it's not too much trouble."

"Not at all. He'll be there Friday at seven." I reach into my purse and produce a credit card. I swallow hard as the reality of what's currently taking place sets in.

Holy shit, I just booked a date with an escort!

The thought does something to me I can't quite explain. Something life-changing, and I like it.

For the first time in my life, I feel powerful, womanly, and definitely sexy.

"You have a date?" my sister, Rachelle, squeals across the line.

I didn't want to tell her, but I gave Jason the name of her restaurant, and she's going to find out when I request a table for two. I'd rather tell her now to get it out of the way and set the ground rules.

"Don't act so surprised," I murmur, rolling my eyes, not that she can see my annoyance.

"What's he like? Who is he? How did you meet?" She bombards me with questions, exactly like I expected her to.

"Seriously, I'm not going to do this with you," I tell her, shutting her down quickly.

"Then why call me at all about it?" she asks.

"I called because I'm meeting him at your restaurant, and I don't want you to bother us."

"Cami—"

"No, I'm serious, Rach. You can't come to the table."

"But I want—"

"It's a first date, a blind date at that. The last thing I need is my sister to scare him away before anything happens."

"Why bring him to my restaurant, then?"

"It was the first place that came to mind when I set it up—I mean, when we discussed where to have dinner," I say quickly, hoping she didn't catch my slipup. "Besides, if the guy is a total douche, at least I'll be somewhere safe and familiar."

She sighs. "Fine, but you better call me the next morning and spill all the juicy details."

"I'm not sure there'll be any to give you." I laugh nervously. Telling Rachelle that I hired an escort to take me out on a date is the last thing I'll ever do. Nope. As far as she's concerned, the date went terrible and I never plan to see him again.

At least part of my lie will be true.

I don't plan on ever seeing him again.

Three

BEN

After picking the girls up from the library, I dropped them off at their mother's, like I do every Thursday afternoon, and headed back to work. I guess you could say I'm a little bit of a workaholic, but running your own company isn't an easy task.

When the economy crashed, I was on the verge of bankruptcy and about to lose everything, including my house. The life and stability I'd worked so hard to build after my divorce was crumbling down around me. I was drowning in debt, with no lifeline in sight. It seemed like no matter how hard I worked, I couldn't get ahead.

Then Jason, an old college buddy, called, and he gave me an offer I couldn't refuse.

He was in a bind and had heard of my divorce. He needed a filler for his new venture. I wasn't surprised to find out Jason was running an escort service out of his family's butcher shop; I knew he'd spent a summer wining and dining women of all ages during college.

His Louisiana Hot Link canceled an hour before he was due to meet up with a client. No one else was available to fill in, and the client was a V.I.P. who couldn't reschedule, so he called me. Since I wasn't serious about any of the women in my life, I saw no harm in helping out a friend. And I didn't have to do anything I didn't want to.

I met up with the client, wined her, dined her, and afterwards, I followed her back to her place, and we fucked like champions. The whole experience was something out of the pages of Playboy, and the best part was the pocket full of cash I went home with. Maybe I shouldn't have been that comfortable with what I was doing, but money talks, especially when you need to make ends meet.

The gig became permanent when the guy I filled in for got stupid with Jason and lost his spot with the service. I didn't hesitate when Jason asked me to step in permanently. My experience that night was a good one, and it's all it took to convince me to become the new Louisiana Hot Link on his menu.

The piercing sound of my cell phone fills the small trailer I've called an office for far too long. I glance down at the screen and see Jason's number flashing back at me.

Speak of the devil!

Looking over at the calendar hanging on the wall, I check to see what the date is. It's Thursday, not my usual night to entertain a date. I wonder if he's calling to ask me to pick up another client, not that I'm in the mood to do so. Seeing Cami today has me all twisted up inside, and the last thing I want to do is spend any time with another woman.

"What's up, Jason?" I answer, knowing there isn't a reason not to answer but all the same racking my brain, trying to figure out what excuse I can use to turn him down.

"Hey, Ben, how're you doing? How are the girls?"

"All is well. How are things with you?"

"Pretty good. Listen, I was wondering if you have any plans tomorrow night?"

And there it is. Pleasantries don't last too long; they never do with Jason, at least not when it comes to the business.

"I don't have anything on the books and nothing happening otherwise. Does one of my regulars need to switch their night?" I ask, hoping it isn't a last-minute booking. We get our schedule on Mondays when we all meet up at The Brown Bottle. But my schedule hasn't changed in months, so he knows my Friday is clear. Jason doesn't usually schedule last-minute bookings, so this is out of character for him.

"No, it's dinner with a new client."

Shit, fuck, shit. I pinch the bridge of my nose.

"I don't know, man. I'm not really in the mood to take on a last-minute booking, let alone a newbie."

"I know, man, but believe me when I say you're going to want this one."

It isn't the first time Jason's given me that line; in fact, it's the line that got me this gig in the first place. But it's also something he says whenever he wants me to pick up a new client. Thankfully, I can choose if I want to take on a new client, regardless of their order.

"I honestly don't have the time to fit another one in. I'm already booked four evenings a week."

"Do you want to know who it is?"

"You said she's new."

"She is, but that doesn't mean you can't know who she is."

"Please, tell me it's not Veronica." I'm praying like hell it isn't my ex-wife. The last thing I need is for her to find out what I do when I don't have the girls.

"What the fuck, man? You think I'd do that to you? Besides, last I heard, she was pretty happy with Bill." He pauses, letting my brain come back from the path I started down. "Do you want to know who it is or not?"

"It doesn't matter who it is. I don't want to take on another client right now."

"Not even Cami?" he asks, chuckling across the line. I choke, unable to respond because I'm not sure if I heard him correctly. "That's fine, Ben. I'll see if Damian's free. I'm sure your girl will enjoy an evening with him."

"What the fuck—" My body locks when he says Damian's name and then calls her mine in the next sentence. The instinct to beat on my chest and mark my territory surges through me.

"She had no idea who she wanted to order, it being her first time with us. Did you know she was *that* shy? She stood at the counter shaking like a leaf. I thought she was going to pass out before she could muster the courage to ask about our extra services."

"You're lying."

"No, man, I'm not. Camilla Babcock, the librarian, the one you told me about after that city job you did. I thought you were kidding when you described her. She's fucking gorgeous," he informs me, trying his hardest to rile me up. He knows who Cami is and what she means to me.

"Jas," I growl into the phone. There's no way he's talking about my Cami. "Shut the fuck up."

"Hell, if I didn't already have plans, I'd take her out myself, find out how those legs feel wrapped around my waist."

"The fuck you will—"

"Damian will show her a good time. She'll get her money's worth. Don't worry, Ben. She'll be in good hands," he barrels on, ignoring my attempts to get a word in. There's no way I'm going to let anyone near Cami, and if they attempt it, I can't promise they'll leave standing up.

"Fuck that. Damian isn't touching her. Matter of fact, he even looks at her, and he'll need to clear his calendar for the next two weeks. He won't be servicing anyone. And don't you have Rocio to worry about?" I growl into the phone, my blood boiling hot in my veins. "When's the fucking setup and where?"

"Ben, it's okay, buddy. We got this—" he starts, ignoring my jab about Rocio.

"Jas, shut the fuck up, man. I'm taking the date."

"I'd thought you'd be happier about this. I thought you liked this woman."

"Not gonna talk about this with you. Just send me a text with everything I need to know." I exhale loudly, pushing out the irritation he built up inside me. My mind is spinning.

My Cami.

My beautiful goddess hired an escort.

And I'm the man for the job.

Four

CAMI

When Jason called me this morning to confirm my date, he told me which special he ordered for me. The Louisiana Hot Link. I'm not sure what it means since I didn't see the menu, but I hope I don't regret trusting him to choose for me.

Sitting at the table of my favorite restaurant, I can't remember a time when I felt this nervous. Not even on my wedding day.

It's just a date, I tell myself. *With an escort!*

I take a deep breath and remind myself that no one else knows that last little bit but me. No one ever has to know either, not even my nosey older sister, who keeps peeking her head out from the kitchen, hoping to catch a glimpse of my date. I groan loudly, fiddling with my half-empty wine glass. I should have chosen another restaurant to meet up.

I'm not worried about my plans tonight. Thanks to Jason's advice, I'm waiting to make any decisions regarding what happens after dinner. While sex isn't off the table, I'm opting to get to know my guy first. I don't need to add any more pressure tonight.

Nervously adjusting the napkin in my lap once again, I'm looking down at my hands when he approaches the table.

"Camilla?" The way he says my name sends a familiar jolt of electricity through my body. Swallowing hard, I look up at him from beneath my lashes, and my heart stops in my chest. Dark chocolate eyes stare down at me, the very same eyes I secretly hoped would be the ones I'm here to meet.

"Ben?" I gasp. *What is he doing here?*

"How are you doing?" He looks down at me with a smirk before pulling out the chair across from me and sitting down.

"Um, I'm waiting for someone," I tell him and quickly scan the room, hoping my date doesn't walk up at this moment. Allowing my eyes to finally settle on him, I notice the dark suit jacket and can't help wondering if he's here with someone. My heart aches a little at the thought of him with someone else, but I push the feeling aside, reminding myself of the reason why I'm here.

"A date?" he asks with a teasing smile, the same one he gives me every time I see him. Sometimes I wonder if he uses it to hide a secret or something.

"Yes, a date," I clip, not wanting to share anything more with him, wishing he'd get up and leave.

"I have a date as well, in case you were wondering." He leans forward, picks up my glass of wine, and sniffs it, like he's some kind of wine connoisseur. "This is a good year. I'm a beer drinker, but I can appreciate a good vintage."

"Hm." I sit back in my chair and take him in. Ben has been a mystery to me since the first time I saw him. But it's his mysteriousness that draws me to him. There is something about him that always puts me at ease when I'm around him. I've never felt this way around another man, and it doesn't hurt that he's panty-melting gorgeous. But I'm here tonight for a reason, and as much as I like Ben, now is not the time to get lost in the magic of what ifs with him. "Look, I don't mean to be rude, but I really am waiting for someone."

"Are you asking me to leave?"

"I thought you said you have a date. Won't she be mad to find you talking with another woman?"

"I don't know. I'll have to ask her."

"Ben—"

"Would you be mad if you found *your* date chatting with another woman?" he questions, leaning back in his chair. It's a curious question, one that shouldn't matter, but I give it some thought before answering.

"It depends. This being my first date with him, probably not."

"Is this a blind date?" He raises an eyebrow, and I shrug.

"If you must know, yes, it's a blind date." I'm not sure what it matters, but I'm not going to give him much more information than that. The last thing I want him to learn is exactly how my date came to be. I need him to leave before my date arrives.

"Please tell me you know what this guy looks like, at least. What if he's some kind of dog?"

"I don't know what he looks like, but I'm pretty sure he isn't a dog," I snip, getting irritated with his line of questions.

"How do you know he hasn't been here already?"

"Why would you say that?" I ask, but his words strike me in the gut. It's a thought I had briefly this morning, after my confirmation call with Jason, but I pushed it aside, ignoring the way it made me doubt myself. Now, thanks to Ben, the thought is back, and this time, there is no ignoring it. I glance down at my watch. My date is fifteen minutes late.

What if Ben's right? What if my date has already been here, saw me, and left because I didn't meet his expectations? Can he do that? Jason never mentioned a standard for his men to date me.

"You're taking my suggestion wrong." He shifts forward and grabs my hand, pulling me from the disastrous thoughts now filling my head.

"What are you doing? I told you—" I try to pull my hand away from his, ignoring the tingles his skin touching mine creates, but he tightens his hold, refusing to let me go.

"Cami, I'm your date," he says quickly, and my eyes fly to his, widening at his omission.

"You're my—"

"I'm the Louisiana Hot Link."

BEN

"You can't be," Cami whispers, and her face falls. She looks at me shocked and worried, trying to piece everything together but unable to comprehend it all.

She looks different from the woman in the library. Her hair is down, and it's longer than I imagined, hitting her at the middle of her back. Her clothes are tighter, more revealing of her sexy body. Her strapless dress has me wishing she'd worn a sweater. From the moment I walked through the door of the restaurant and my eyes found her alone at the table, I was hard. Uncomfortably hard.

What I've learned in the short time I've known her is that I like Cami, in all shapes and forms, and seeing her tonight, her skirt showing more thigh than I've ever seen from her, I can't stop thinking about those legs being wrapped around my waist as I pound into her, making her scream my name.

"Why can't I be?" I clear my throat, shifting my body so my hard cock is hidden underneath the table.

"Because," she says, lowering her voice to a harsh whisper and leaning forward a little. "My date is—"

"An escort?" I watch as her chest concaves with the air exiting her body because the shock of my words is almost too much for her. Cami doesn't seem like the kind of woman who needs to pay for a date, but if there is one thing I've learned in this business, looks are deceiving. "I work for Jason, babe. I'm your date. *Your* Louisiana Hot Link."

Her mouth flaps open and closed a few times, and she blindly blinks at me. My chest aches, and for the first time tonight, I realize I might not be what she is expecting. A divorced father of two who works too much, reads suspense thrillers, and takes women out because they pay him to. I must look like a real winner to her. I let go of her hand, suddenly very self-conscious.

"Ben—" she starts, but I stop her, unable to handle her rejection.

"Look, don't say anything yet." I sigh, raking my hand through my hair, thankful I didn't use any hair product tonight. "I can see I'm not what you were expecting, so if you want, I'll call Jason and have him schedule someone else for you."

Mine. The thought of another man with her angers me, but I have to consider what she wants, too. We've never gotten to the point where I could stake a claim on her, but given the chance to ever do so, I would in a heartbeat.

I shift my body, getting ready to stand, but she reaches out and grabs my hand, keeping me in my seat. I look at her, and the moment our eyes connect, her entire demeanor changes. She relaxes, and the worry I felt vanishes.

"Stay." Her voice is soft and gentle, but I still see confusion in her eyes.

"Cami, I'm sorry if I'm not what you expected. I don't want to disappoint you," I tell her honestly because it's the last thing I want to do. "I wouldn't have taken this appointment, but Jason..." I trail off, unable to tell her why Jason really wanted me to be her date.

"Did you know it was me?"

"Yes." I nod.

"But you came anyways."

"Yes."

"I don't understand. Why?"

"Does it bother you? Me knowing it was you tonight." I ignore the "why" because it will make things too complicated right now.

"I guess not. It's just... I never would have thought you were... That you did this kind of thing." I laugh lightly, watching her cheeks flush from my reaction. "I mean, not that I'm judging you or anything, but you're a good-looking guy—"

"I shouldn't have to *escort* beautiful women?"

"I didn't mean to imply—" She slaps her hands over her mouth, making me laugh louder this time. "What you do on your dates—"

"Cami, it's okay." I reach across the table and grasp her hands, trying to calm her. "I take it you didn't look over the menu?"

"I didn't," she breathes, her body tense and wound up. We both fall silent and sit staring at each other, trying to figure out what to do next. Being the gentleman the menu describes me as, I wait for her to decide what happens next, even though my instinct to reach across the table and kiss her senseless boils under the surface.

I hope she decides to stay, to pursue this, because I want this woman. More than any other woman I've ever been with. The idea of finding myself between her glorious long legs tonight, tasting her, fucking her, had me relieving myself more than once before my arrival.

Not that it helped; the tightness in my pants tells me as much.

"So, what now?" she asks, tucking a stray piece of hair behind her ear.

"It's your call." I can't help the smile that slips onto my face as I imagine running my hand through her dark silky hair, gripping it at the roots for a little tug. I wonder if she'll purr or growl from the action. She eyes me carefully, fingering her glass of wine.

"What's your description on the menu?"

"Louisiana Hot Link. Ben, age forty-one, brown hair and brown eyes. Always the gentleman, Ben will remind you how a woman is supposed to be treated. With arms thick and strong, he'll wrap them around you and make you feel safe and protected."

She smiles brightly. "A gentleman?"

"I try to be."

She lifts her glass to her lips and drains it. I glance around, looking for the waiter to refill it for her, but there is no one around. In fact, I find it odd that no one has bothered approaching for a drink order since I sat down.

"I asked them to stay away," she explains, reading my mind. "My sister owns the place, and I asked her to make sure no one approached us unless I summoned them."

"I see. Would you like more wine?"

She pauses, contemplating her choice.

"No." Her voice is soft, but her eyes have turned golden. "What if I don't want you to be a gentleman?"

I lift an eyebrow, watching the way her face flushes

and her chest puffs as her breathing rate increases. She's feeling braver now.

"I can be whatever you want me to be, Cami." I lower my voice and narrow my eyes on her, watching the way my words physically affect her. She shivers, and her nipples harden, peeking at me from underneath her dress. Her tongue flicks out and runs across her lower lip. I hold back the urge to throw her over my shoulder and carry her out of here.

Five

CAMI

L ord, help me, I don't want him to be a gentleman. We've been playing cat and mouse for too long, and I want to take advantage of the moment.

Yes, I was shocked to discover he was my date, that he was an escort, but I'm not unhappy about it. I'm actually excited, and for the first time since deciding to do this, I'm completely comfortable. But he's always had this effect on me.

"How does this usually work?" I ask, suddenly wanting to skip dinner and take him to my place and realizing the part of the evening I was most unsure about is now the one I want the most. I take a deep breath, trying to calm my insides.

It's because it's with him, my mind whispers, and as much as I want to deny it, I can't. It's true.

"Usually, dinner first, and then whatever a client wants." He tilts his head and places a hand on the table next to mine. His fingers close the distance and gently stroke my fingers. "But, Cami, you are anything but usual."

I try to hold back my reaction, but it's difficult, especially when he says things like that.

"Are you hungry?" My heart beats wildly in my chest.

"Yes." He smirks, and his eyes glitter at me with need. "But not for anything they serve here."

Oh my…

I press my thighs together, trying to ignore the wetness now soaking my panties. The Ben I've known all along still prominent in my head only makes this moment even more exciting. As much as I like that Ben, I'm falling pretty quickly for this new side of him.

"Cami, do you want to get out of here?"

"Your place or mine?" I respond without hesitation.

"Yours," he breathes, making me think about the fresh sheets I put on my bed this morning.

"Are you able to drive?" I frown, but he explains. "How much wine have you had, Cami?"

"Three glasses," I answer, suddenly wondering if that's why I'm feeling brave with him.

"I'll settle the check. Leave your keys with the valet, and I'll drive you over in the morning to get your car," he tells me, not really giving me an option.

"Ben, I can drive." He stands up, places both hands onto the table, and leans into me. I swallow hard as the scent of him surrounds me, intoxicating me until I no longer feel the effects of the wine because I'm drunk off him and this moment.

"I want you in my truck, Cami. I want to smell you

as I drive to your house. I want to see the look on your face when you think about the things I'm going to do to you. I want to reach across and touch you." I squirm in my seat, no longer worried about the people around us or even my nosey sister watching us from the kitchen. He chuckles throatily and offers me his hand. "Good, now stand up and let's get out of here."

I take his hand and stand. His jaw tightens as he takes in the sight of me in my new strapless mini dress and fuck-me heels. I'm tall, especially in these heels, but the man in front of me makes me feel tiny and delicate. I let him take all of what I have to offer in, enjoying the effect it has on him.

"Fuck, Cami, what you are wearing?" He steps in front of me, placing himself between me and the rest of the room. His eyes narrow on me, and he reaches down to adjust himself. I can't help it; my eyes travel down the length of his body, stopping at his hard cock. A chill runs through my body knowing I'm the cause of it.

"Too much, if you really want to know." I laugh and move around him. He places a hand on my waist and follows close behind me. I stop in my tracks and feel the brush of his hard-on against my ass when he tries not to ram into me. "We both are."

I hear him groan and smile inwardly. *Score one for the librarian.*

He follows me to the hostess, where he settles the bill. Hand in hand, we leave the restaurant, and I give my ticket to the valet, quickly explaining what the plan is. I also send a text to my sister, telling her I'll stop by in the morning for my car. I already know the barrage of messages I'll likely wake up to. She'll want a full report; after all, it isn't every day her baby sister meets a date at her restaurant and leaves without eating.

Ben leads me into the parking lot, and I spot his truck immediately. It stands out like a sore thumb amongst the sea of luxury vehicles. We barely make it to the truck before he grabs me, spins us both, and pins me against the passenger side.

His hands cup my face a second before his lips find mine, and a hungry growl emanates from his chest. It's a demanding kiss, one meant to mark and claim. I open my mouth, pushing my tongue into his, deepening the kiss, moaning over his minty taste.

I lift my hands and push aside his suit jacket to find the soft fabric of his button-up shirt. I shiver, picturing what the muscle underneath my fingers looks like, needing to feel the heat of his skin pressed against me. He lets the jacket slide off him and to the ground.

One less piece to remove later, I think as his hands release my face and make their way slowly down my body until his fingers brush against my naked thigh. He hooks one hand under my knee, and his other holds at my waist. I hike my leg up, instinctively wrapping it around him, granting him further access while he pushes up my skirt. He settles himself between my legs and surges against me, grinding his hard, hot length against me.

"Fuck," I moan, enjoying the feeling of him against me.

"Babe..." He pulls away, leaving me gasping for

breath. He places his forehead against mine, his hands still holding my body tightly. "Need to get you home."

I respond by pushing my hips into him, grinding even harder against his cock. I need him just as bad.

"So, get me home."

He groans and reluctantly pushes off me. When he opens his eyes and finally looks down at me, I see desire burning there. The same desire I feel burning throughout my body.

BEN

The drive to her house is excruciating. More so because of the faces she makes when her eyes dart from me to the road. I know what she's thinking. What she's picturing. Because I'm thinking the same.

The kiss wasn't something I'd planned. It was something I needed. It was the kind of kiss that told me everything I need to know about the woman sitting next to me and the dynamite night we are bound to have. I can still taste her cherry-flavored lip gloss.

She directs me to her house with ease, and it surprises me to find out how close we live to one another. The world keeps getting smaller and smaller. Her bungalow is similar to my own.

"This is me," she breathes, and I pull into the driveway. I put the truck in park and look over at her. She's nervous. More than she was earlier at the restaurant.

"We don't have to do this, Cami." I turn toward her,

reaching for a hand and giving it a little squeeze. "I'll take you back to your car."

Her brown eyes soften on me before fire begins to slowly burn in their depths. "I'm not going to change my mind."

She opens her car door and slides out of the truck, leaving me at a loss for words. The timid Cami I know is suddenly a smoking vixen. I scramble out of the truck, quick to follow her lead. We stop on her porch as she fishes through her purse for her keys. Her bright yellow door glows in the dark of the night, its color reflecting her friendly personality. I like it.

She opens the door, and I follow her inside, kicking it closed behind me. I'm no longer able to keep my hands to myself. I reach for her and press myself against her back. She responds by pushing her ass harder against my cock, moaning loudly when my hands cup her breasts over her dress. Her nipples harden under my touch.

"Fuck, babe, you're responsive." I slip my hand into the top of her dress, finding her nipples instantly. She arches into my touch. My lips find her neck, and I run my tongue along the column up to her ear.

"Ben..." she purrs, letting me hear the need in her voice. She grabs my thighs tightly. Her fingernails bite through my slacks, making me harder. "More..."

I grip her shoulders and turn her quickly before pinning her against the nearest wall. Pictures fall from the force of our bodies knocking into it, but we ignore them. I push her skirt up and lift her, cupping her ass.

She wraps her legs around me like a vise, and I press my throbbing cock against her core.

I nearly come in my pants. The heat of her body makes me spin. Having her like this, sandwiched between me and the wall, is a dream come true. Everything about her—her scent, her taste, the feeling of her body pressed against me—is better than anything I can dream up. Our lips meet in a hurried but deep kiss. I send up a silent prayer of thanks to whatever fate put us together tonight.

Her hands are warm on my chest, and her fingers push and pull at the buttons on my shirt until it's open and off my shoulders. Her hands touch my bare skin, sending a bolt of electricity shooting through me, making my cock throb.

"Babe." I pull back, holding on to her like my life depends on it. "As much as I want to fuck you against the wall, the first time I have you, I want to take my time."

"Ben," she moans, her eyes half-lidded with desire. She snakes her arms around my neck, kissing and licking along my jawline.

"Bedroom?" My hands grip her ass tightly when I move away from the wall, and I carry her down the hallway.

"End of the hallway," she murmurs. Her heels hit the floor as we go, and her legs tighten around me.

I push open the door at the end of the hall and enter her bedroom. The scent of vanilla and lavender surrounds me, and I note the neutral tones covering the walls, her furniture, and bedding. After laying her down on the bed, I push her skirt up around her waist, and I groan loudly at the sight of her blue lace panties. They barely cover her pussy. I'm not a man who likes lingerie, but for this woman, I'm willing to change that aspect, especially if her closet is filled with items like these.

Looking up at me with lust-filled eyes, she reaches for me, but I grab her wrists and pin her hands above her head.

"Don't move, Cami." I capture her lips with my own and swallow her husky moan. My hands travel down her body, and when I reach her legs, I brush my finger-tips along her inner thighs.

"Please," she begs, thrusting her hips up, but I continue on course, teasing her soft, silky skin. I trail my lips down her neck and pull her top down with my teeth, revealing two dusty pink rosebuds just waiting for my mouth to claim them. I flick my tongue over one of the sensitive buds, once, twice, before sucking it into my mouth. She arches her back, giving me better access to them.

I slip one hand between her legs, and I trace the line of her pussy through the delicate lace, groaning loudly at the way my fingers slide along the material. She's fucking soaked. I kiss and lick her creamy skin, stop-ping at the top of her panties. I pause and meet her gaze. She's holding her breath, waiting and watching me. I breathe in deeply, inhaling her sweet scent.

Mine.

She opens her legs to me, the anticipation too much,

and she thrusts her hips forward. I know what she wants.

"Patience, beautiful. I'll get there." I chuckle and kneel on the floor beside the bed, pulling her to the edge and spreading her legs even further. After hooking a finger in the delicate material of her panties, I pull at it, ripping them from her body. Her pretty pussy glistens up at me, and I lower my head and kiss along her inner thigh, biting her flesh.

"Ben," she pants, tensing each time my lips move and don't make contact where she needs them most. I smile, loving the power I hold over her. It's intoxicating.

I pull back for only a moment before placing my mouth over her clit, flicking it with my tongue before sucking the swollen bud into my mouth. Her body quivers from the pressure, and she lets out a hiss as I release it from between my teeth. I slide a finger into her tight warmth and continue to lap and tease her bundle of nerves until she's gasping for breath.

"Don't stop," she pants. Her fists grip the sheet above her head like it's her lifeline. Sensing how close she is to the edge, I slip a second finger inside her, stretching her tightness. I groan, wishing I were already plunging balls deep inside her.

Six

CAMI

He slips in a third finger, filling and stretching me until I don't think I can take any more. I welcome the feeling, knowing soon I'll take more. I felt the size of him pressed firmly against me in the parking lot. My guess is, I'm going to feel him for days.

Ben nips at my clit, grazing his teeth against it. The sensation winds me tighter. I'm desperate to come. Flattening his warm tongue against me, he thrusts his fingers in and out, driving me to the point of no return.

"Please," I beg, needing him to push me over the edge. He smirks up at me before granting me mercy and clamping down, sucking my bud into his mouth. I shoot off like a rocket as my orgasm hits me full force. He replaces his fingers with his tongue, assaulting my clit with a slippery finger. The sensation is unlike anything I've ever felt before.

"Ben!" I yell, convulsing around his tongue. Our eyes connect, and a new wave hits me. This time, I relax, my body tingles, and my breath hitches. It makes me question why I waited so long to be with someone.

Never again, I vow, my brain barely able to function. He begins to slow his assault on my clit, letting me gradually come down from the intense pleasure. My body feels reenergized, and as satisfying as that was, it wasn't what I want most.

I curl forward and reach for him. He follows my lead and climbs up the length of my body, briefly settling over me. I kiss him hastily, tasting the remnants of my orgasm on his tongue.

"You're glowing," he whispers, looking down at me with awe.

"It's been a while since I've felt like this." I laugh, pushing at his shoulders and shoving him onto his back. I straddle him and pull my dress over my head, tossing it somewhere behind me. "You ruined my panties."

"I'll buy you new ones." His voice is husky, filled with need.

I make my way down his chiseled chest, kissing and nipping as I go. It isn't until I reach his belt buckle and slowly release him from the confines of his clothing, that I truly understand the sheer size of him.

Holy shit, he's huge. At least eight inches, but it isn't his length I find most shocking. I reach down to wrap my hand around him, but my fingers are nowhere near touching.

"Don't worry. I'll fit." I look up to find him staring down at me. He chuckles because my wide-eyed stare gives away my thoughts. He lifts himself, allowing me to pull his jeans and boxer briefs down past his hips. I remove his shoes and finish pulling off the rest of his clothing.

Shaking of my initial shock, I move closer to him and run my tongue over the head of his cock. Wound tight like a rubber band, ready to snap at a moment's notice, his body shudders from the sensation. I place a soft kiss over the same spot, watching his cock twitch from the sensation.

"You don't have to do that, Cami." His voice is strangled, like he's having a hard time focusing. I love seeing him this way.

"I want to taste you." My voice is a whisper. Opening my mouth, I swipe my tongue along the underside of his cock, sucking him as far down my throat as I can. When he hits the back of my throat, I adjust myself, taking on more. He groans, hands thread through my hair, and he grips it at the root, stopping me from going any further.

"Babe, I'm not going to last." I snicker, wanting him to lose control, so I can swallow every drop of him I can get. "We have all night. As much as I want to come from that sweet mouth of yours, I need to feel you milk my cock with that tight pussy more."

Smiling inwardly, I comply, rising up from my position to straddle him. I place him at my entrance, but before I can move, he grips my hips.

"Condom." The word is like a bucket of ice, but his brown eyes never waver, keeping me in the moment.

Shit, what was I thinking almost taking him bareback? He lifts me up and settles me off to the side. He grabs his jeans and takes out a silver foil packet from one of the pockets. I lean back on the bed, watching as he rips it open with his teeth and slides the rubber down his large shaft. I swallow hard, and wetness surges between my legs.

He moves, hovering over me for a moment, catching my eyes. He lifts a hand and caresses my cheek with such tenderness, it leaves my heart aching in my chest. I see warmth in his eyes, behind the need, and I let myself embrace it. His hardness presses at my entrance again. I open for him, wrapping my legs around his middle.

"Ben." My voice is gentle, dripping with need I've never felt before. He lowers his head and catches my lips before slowly surging forward with his hips. I've never experienced a slow burn, but this has to be what it feels like. He shifts, holding one hand at my hips, keeping me from moving, and the other hand supporting his weight. He slowly fills me, stretching me so tight, I feel desperate for more. "Please, more..."

He ignores my plea, holding my hip tighter, refusing to let me speed up the moment. His sac hits me, and I know I've taken all he can give. He starts to pull out, just as slowly as he started. I try moving, pushing forward, but he doesn't let me.

"Been dreaming of this moment for too long, Cami. Want it to last as long as I can make it," he tells me, reading the tension in my body. Slow and steady, he builds me up.

I moan loudly. The sensation of his cock pushing in and out of me is almost more than I can handle. He doesn't relent, keeping pace and trapping me in a slow burn.

BEN

Even though I'm the hot link on the menu, I prefer a slow and steady burn. Spicy doesn't always mean hard and fast.

The way her pussy grips my cock hard, it takes everything in me to keep it slow and steady because all I want to do is pound away at her sweetness. If she hadn't told me it's been a while for her, I would throw caution to the wind and have my way with her. But I can tell by the way her greedy pussy sucks me in, she's telling the truth. The further I push into her, the tighter she gets, and the last thing I want to do is hurt her.

"Fuck, Cami, you feel like heaven," I mumble, slipping a hand between us to find her clit. She purrs in the back of her throat, clearly approving my efforts. "Need you to come."

"Need you to speed up, so I can."

"You first," I challenge, increasing the speed and pressure I hold over her sensitive bud. Her body tenses, trying to hold out, but the moment her eyes fly open, I know she can't fight me anymore. She explodes around my cock, clamping down on me so hard, it takes all my restraint not to come.

My name on her lips never sounded so good, but while she's flying high, I gradually pick up speed, adjusting my position to hit her G-spot, prolonging her pleasure. I release my hold on her hips, finally allowing her to move with me, and she does, urging me to push faster and harder.

"Ben," she breathes, her nails scraping the length of my back. Stuck in the limbo of her orgasm, she can only feel what I give her. "Faster… harder…"

"Come again for me, baby." I gasp as my body tenses, the ache from my balls reminding me I don't have much longer until I lose control. Fighting off my own pleasure, I focus solely on the woman underneath me and give her what she asks for.

Harder and faster. The slow burn is gone, replaced with need unlike anything I've ever felt before.

The need to claim her.

The need to make her mine in every way possible.

Her body twitches underneath me, and she lets loose a scream of satisfaction, signaling her third and final orgasm. I continue to give her what she wants as pleasure tears through her body, drenching my cock with her sweet nectar.

My fucking goddess.

I know I'm close when the familiar tingle deep in my balls begins. She's clamped so tightly around me, I'm surprised I can move.

But I do move.

Harder. Faster.

One stroke.

Two.

"Fuck…" My body jerks uncontrollably, and I finally find my release. Wave after wave crashes around me until I no longer know where she begins and I end.

Connected as one, we only have each other to hold on to as our pleasure runs its course.

I begin to slow my jerky movements, and she wraps her arms around my neck, placing gentle kisses along my shoulder.

"Cami..." I lower my face to her dark hair, filling my lungs with her scent. There's so much I want to say to her right now, but words elude me as exhaustion seeps in. I've never felt this sated this fast in my life. But I know it won't last long. I'll never be able to get enough of her.

"Ben," she sighs as I pull out of her and collapse beside her. She rolls, places her head on my chest, and drags in a deep, satisfied breath.

Holding her, I get the sense that whatever it is I want to say will have wait because I feel her sated body relax and exhaustion consume her.

Once she is asleep, I slip out of bed and discard the proof of our love-making.

When I finally crawl back in beside her, I cover us both up, loving the fact that I'm falling asleep with her in my arms.

How did I get this lucky?

CAMI

Light filters into the room, waking me to the gentle snore of someone beside me. My body freezes at the sound, but the delicious pull of used muscles reminds me of the events from the previous night and who I'm in bed with.

Ben.

His large, warm body stirs next to me, and I close my eyes, pretending to be asleep. Once he settles, his breath deepening again, I turn my head to take in the sight of him. But instead of finding a sleeping giant, I'm met with a large smile and sleepy brown eyes.

"Good morning," he drawls, and his deep voice sends a thrill through my body.

"Morning," I respond, turning the rest of my body to face him. He lifts an arm, and I snuggle into the crook, placing my hand on his chest to trace the hard lines of muscle. He wraps his arm tightly around me.

The sound of his stomach growling fills the awkward silence growing between us.

"Someone's hungry," I laugh and snuggle into him.

"My date made me skip dinner last night. She couldn't wait for her dessert," he teases. I can feel the smile on his lips as he presses a kiss against my head. "Would you like to get some breakfast?"

"I can't." I look up at him, wishing I could spend the day wrapped in his arms. "I have to work today. Dinner tonight?"

"I've got my girls tonight."

"What about Sunday night, then? I'll make dinner." I lift up and settle on his chest, looking down at him. I lean in to place a gentle kiss on his lips. Usually, I'm a stickler for oral hygiene, but I want to feel his lips on mine more than I care about my morning breath.

"Sunday is no good, babe." He tenses against me, but his arms reach around me, holding me close. It's all I need to know the reason why Sunday is a no-go.

"You have a date," I state. My heart squeezes in my chest, telling me I might have invested more than my body during our time together.

"Yes," he says, squashing any hope that I'm wrong. "I can come by afterwards if you want."

"I don't think that's a good idea." I shake my head and try pushing off him. Does he really believe he can go from his date's bed to mine like that?

"Why not?" he asks. His reluctance to let me go makes me push harder, and he finally releases me. Staring up at me, he seems to be trying to figure out what's happening. I slide off him and onto my back, covering myself with the sheet, trying to shield myself from him. Not that it matters; he's seen every inch of me. "What's going on in that head of yours, Cami?"

"Nothing. Sundays are usually pretty busy for me anyways, prepping for next week and all. I shouldn't have asked." I sit up and look around the room for something, anything, to put on. I need to get out of this bed before I hurl all over myself. The thought of him being with another woman, the way we were only hours ago, makes me sick. I need space to think, to sort out the mess in my head and my heart. His arms snake around my middle, pulling me into the hard nakedness of his chest.

"Are you upset because I have a date?"

"It's okay, Ben. I get it. I'm not your only client." I take a deep breath. My chest hurts too much to keep everything inside. "I just thought after last night…"

He waits for me to continue, but the courage I felt disappears. The reality of who he is and what he does comes crashing down on me. He's an escort; of course there is going to be other women. One night with him doesn't give me claim to him. Besides, I paid for our night together.

"After last night what?" He nudges me, tightening his hold on me. I lean into him, swallowing the hurt itching to spill out of me, remembering I'm just like the others now.

"It doesn't matter, Ben."

"Babe, if it bothers you, it matters." There's gentleness in his voice when he says the words. It eases the pain and calms my churning stomach. "Talk to me."

"I thought maybe I was different. Maybe we were different."

"You *are* different." I don't respond because I don't know how to. If that were true, wouldn't he cancel his dates? "You can come with me."

"Are you crazy? I'm not going on your date with you." Sitting up again, I exhale deeply. *He can't be serious.*

"It's not that kind of date. Come with me. Mrs. Morello would love the extra company."

"Mrs. Morello?"

"Yes, my seventy-two-year-old date. That woman makes killer sauce. But Mrs. Boyle, my Wednesday night date, makes an Irish stew that will make your toes curl."

"I don't understand." I stand, wrapping the sheet tightly around myself, and I turn to face him.

"I told you, it isn't what you think. I'm not what you think." He smirks up at me, the lines of his face soften, and his eyes tell me he's speaking the truth. He reaches for my hand and lifts it to his lips. "I don't fuck for money."

"Then why did I give Jason my credit card number?" I ask, lifting an eyebrow.

"Pomp and circumstance. Check your statement. You'll see he didn't charge you for any of the fees you discussed with him. And he won't." He pulls me into him again, leaning down to place a kiss on the tip of my nose. "Jason called me the moment you left his shop, which he planned to do as soon as you told him your name. He's my best friend, babe. He knows what you are to me."

"What am I to you?"

"Mine." The word sounds like a confession—one that makes me soft on the inside and tingly down south. "You have been since the moment I laid eyes on you. Fucked up when I didn't make my move back then."

"You're joking, right?"

"I'm being serious." He looks down at our connected hands, and I watch his Adam's apple bob as he swallows hard. "You're gorgeous, Cami. Everything a man could possibly want. You're smart. Cute as hell, especially when you don't realize you're being cute. You even do this thing with a pencil, like you're chewing on the end of the eraser, but you're concentrating on something important. When you look up at me with those dark chocolate eyes, I sometimes forget how to breathe. You're everything and more. You're mine."

"Ben—"

"My dates, I can't give those up, Cami. Those women, they depend on me to show up every week." He glances up at me and shows me his concern. "I can see if some of the other guys would be willing to take them on, but it depends on their schedules."

"How many of them are there?" I ask carefully, bracing myself for his answers.

"Four."

"But you don't sleep with any of them?"

He chuckles, maybe because he senses the jealousy brewing inside of me, but it does nothing to help ease it.

"No, babe, I don't sleep with them. But I'm not going to lie. I have slept with clients in the past. No one recent, and it's been a long time since I took on a new client."

"You took me on."

"You're not a client." I find his honesty inspiring and decide to trust him, giving him another piece of me.

"I like you, too. I mean, from the start." I swallow hard, afraid to put myself out there with him but needing to do it. "I was married before. He was a jerk. He hurt me, and since then, I've been cautious. You're the first man to make me feel comfortable, like I'm good enough. I don't have to pretend to be someone I'm not with you."

"I like who you are, Cami. I don't want to be with anyone else."

"I want to be with you, too, Ben." He cups my face and kisses me, wiping away any remaining worries or concerns. "What now?"

"Now, we take it one day at a time," he responds, pulling back a little. "I'm not going anywhere, Cami. I get you got a past. I do, too. But that's all it is. Our past."

"Will you leave The Meat Market?"

"Meeting with the guys on Monday, planned on doing it then."

Feeling brave, I drop the sheet from my chest and turn to straddle him. He pushes my messy hair away from my face and looks at me with adoration in his eyes. "We got some things to work out, but I don't want to think about it anymore, Ben."

"When do you have to be at work?"

"Oh, I don't know. I think I feel a cold coming on." I smile down at him as I wrap my arms and legs around him. Lowering my head, I brush my lips lightly against his, teasing him. "Maybe I should call in sick."

"I think that's the best thing you've said all morning." He reaches up and claims my lips in one swift motion, stealing the breath from my lungs and ultimately my heart.

BEN

"Sweet Cami, I can't begin to tell you how much joy it gives me to see Ben so happy," Mrs. Morello coos from across the table. Cami's hand tightens in mine, and I watch as she relaxes into her chair. It was a fight to get her here tonight, but now that she's met Mrs. Morello, I can sense her relief. "The ladies at the auxiliary club will be thrilled, too."

"That's very kind of you," Cami replies with a warm smile. Her brown eyes shine brightly in Mrs. Morello's dimly-lit kitchen.

"We've all been so worried about him," Mrs. Morello continues, but not before standing and adding more pasta to my plate. She throws me a wink and an extra meatball. "He's been alone for too long. It's high time he finds a woman to share his life with. The ladies and I did everything we could to keep our weekly dates with him, so he had a least three good meals during the week. Do you cook, Cami?"

Cami swings a look my way, but from the frown on

my own forehead, she knows I have no idea what the old woman is talking about.

"I do. Very well, actually. My sister is a chef, and she taught me everything I know."

"Wonderful," Mrs. Morello exclaims with a clap of her hands. "Tonight, before you leave, I will give you my recipe for Ben's favorite meatballs. It was my mother's recipe, but since I never had children of my own, and Ben has become somewhat of a son to me, I'd be happy to pass it on to you. Of course, you'll have to promise to pass it on to your own children. I mean, that is if you plan on having any. Do you?"

"Mrs. Morello—" I start, but Cami gives my hand another squeeze. I've never known the woman to be this intrusive, but then again, I had no idea my weekly date with her was something done strictly to take care of me because I'm not married. Learning that my other two weekly standing dates are based on the same reasoning, I don't know what to think. Here I thought I was doing something good for them.

"One day," Cami answers softly. She keeps her gaze on Mrs. Morello, but her cheeks brighten as she speaks. "I'd like to have children of my own."

"What about you, Ben? I know you have two girls, but would you want more? With Cami?" Mrs. Morello beams, but I know what's she doing here. Most of what she told us tonight might be news to me, but her line of questioning isn't.

"Mrs. Morello, are you trying to play matchmaker?" I ask, smiling at her.

"Guilty," she laughs, throwing up her hands.

"As I've told you in the past, with the right woman, I'd love to have more children," I answer, looking at Cami and meeting her gaze. I let her see the truth behind my words.

The right woman.

Her.

The soft look in her eyes strikes me in the chest. She feels it, too.

"Do you hear that, girl?" Cami nods but doesn't look away. "What do you think about my sweet Ben here?"

"I think he's… very special," she answers, finally breaking her gaze and looking at Mrs. Morello. I watch as she smiles, giving the old woman the same warm smile she's given me time after time.

I've never wanted a woman like I want her. I'd give her babies and have fun making them. As many as she wants. I want them to have her brown eyes, natural wit, and love of books. I want her to be a part of Kinsley and Katie's life, and not just as the librarian they work with.

"Well, would you look at that," Mrs. Morello coos, sitting back in her chair to take in the sight of Cami's heated blush and my inability to look away from the beautiful creature beside me. "Looks like this is going to be my last Sunday night dinner, Benjamin."

CAMI

I kiss Ben one last time before wrapping my robe around me and exiting the room in search of my cell phone. We both fell asleep after another fantastic night. But I was woken moments ago by the sound of my phone going off for what has to be the hundredth time tonight.

My sister, despite the multiple text messages I've sent, reassuring her of my wellbeing has refused to stop calling me. I know if I don't call her back soon, she'll be pounding on my door looking for better answers.

I close the door softly behind me and make my way toward the front of my house, dialing her number as I go.

"It's about fucking time you called me back. You're too late, though. I'm walking up to your front door right now."

"No, Rachelle, you can't come here," I panic, freezing mid-step to look around the room. Ben's clothing, along with my own, trails from the front door down the hall to my bedroom.

"Too late," she replies, hanging up on me and knocking on my front door. The sound of her knock jolts me out of my panic, and I scramble to pick up the proof of my weekend activities. Except for last night—when he had the girls—and dinner with Mrs. Morello, we've spent our time exploring one another without clothing.

Rachelle knocks again, this time louder. "I know you're home, Cami. You said as much on the phone."

Throwing the large pile of clothing into the spare room, I look around one last time for any sign of Ben. Seeing none, I take a breath and walk over to the door to let my sister in.

"I told you I was fine." I open the door, not bothering to mask my annoyance at her presence.

"And you promised me the juicy details in exchange for privacy Friday night." She pushes past me and heads into the kitchen. "It's Sunday, and I have no juicy details. What gives?"

I watch as she reaches into my refrigerator and cracks open a bottle of water. She chugs it, and I realize she's decked out in her running gear and looks like she just ran a marathon.

"Did you run here?"

"Yup," she gasps, using the back of her arm to wipe the sweat off her upper lip. "Spill."

I glance down the hall, hoping she doesn't see me do it, before answering. "Rachelle, it's really not a good time for this."

"Why not? I thought you said you were okay?" She looks me up and down, her eyes searching for something to be wrong with me.

"I am, but I was about to jump in the shower." I tighten my robe around me and flick my head to the back bedroom, hoping she'll get the hint and go.

She looks at me, her brow puckering in confusion. "You're kicking me out because you were getting ready to take a shower?"

"I'm not kicking you out," I argue, lowering my voice a little. The last thing I need is for her to wake Ben. I'm not ready to tell my sister anything about him, but she catches on to the level of my voice, my appearance, and my cagey behavior.

"Oh, my God, he's here, isn't he?" she asks, her eyes

wide with shock and awe. "You dirty little slut... Wait, is it the same guy? The one from Friday night?"

"Wow, who do you think I am? Yes, it's the same guy." I scowl, crossing my arms.

"I think you're a grown-ass woman who has every right to explore life as she pleases." Rachelle cocks an eyebrow and smirks. "And if he's who you're exploring life with, well, then I'm one jealous bitch."

I feel an arm slip around my waist as Ben steps up behind me. "Everything all right in here?" he asks. His deep voice fills the air, sending a shiver through my body. I look up at him, in awe of the way he's looking at my sister without a sliver of the annoyance I feel toward her. He's poised to protect but without being an ass about it.

Will I ever get enough of this man? I wonder to myself.

"You must be Cami's sister."

"Yes, I'm Rachelle," she flounders, reaching out a hand to him. He takes her hand without letting his hold on me go.

"Nice to meet you, Rachelle. I'm Ben," he replies nonchalantly, giving her a devilish grin. Rachelle looks the Adonis behind me up and down before stopping on me. She's dumbstruck and absolutely speechless. Her jaw flaps as she struggles to form words, but nothing comes.

She looks to me, but I'm enjoying seeing her struck like this. It reminds me of the first day I laid eyes on him and how he made me feel.

Ben has that kind of effect on women, and he has no idea of it. He's always too busy to notice the way women turn to look at him as he walks by. The way they stare and murmur behind his back.

"Can I have my hand back?" Ben asks, interrupting my thoughts, and I see Rachelle snatch her hand back, shocked at the indecent time she spent holding his.

"Ben, do you think you can give me a moment with Rachelle?" I ask, turning in his arms and reaching up to kiss him lightly on the lips.

"Sure," he murmurs before stepping back and nodding to my sister. "It was nice meeting you, Rachelle. I'm sure I'll be seeing you again."

She nods dumbly, but the moment he's out of sight, she's on me.

"Holy fucking shit," she swears in a harsh whisper. "Do you know who he is?"

Shit.

All my blood freezes in my veins, and for the first time since walking into The Meat Market, I realize my sister might know all about the place and the men who are a part of it. She does own one of the hottest restaurants in the city.

"Yes, he's the architect who did the renovations on the library I was telling you about," I answer, hoping it's enough to sway her away from his other job.

"You're kidding me. That's the Adonis?"

"Yes, why?"

"So, he doesn't work for Jason Somers at that butcher shop?"

"I have no idea what you're talking about, Rachelle," I say, but her eyes light up a second later.

"I thought you said he was a blind date—"

"Rach—"

"Oh, my God, you went down there and booked a date with them, didn't you?" Instead of being shocked at my behavior, Rachelle has the biggest smile plastered across her face.

"It isn't like that with him—"

"I bet they all say that—"

"No, it isn't." Ben's voice rounds the corner, and he pins my sister in place with a cold stare. "Yes, I used to offer services at Jason's shop, but I haven't taken on a new client in a long time. Until Cami."

"Until Cami?" she asks.

"Jason is one of my best friends, has been since college. He knew about Cami the first day I met her, and he called me the second she walked out of his shop." He wraps an arm around my waist and pulls me hard against him. I feel the tension in his body. "I was going to ask Cami out the next time I saw her, already had it planned, but fate had another plan for us. Guess I wasn't moving fast enough for it."

"I didn't mean to insinuate—"

"I'm guessing you didn't, but I've been to your restaurant a time or two with a client, and I thought it best this came from me and not Cami. I have a past, one I'm not exactly proud of, but I did what I had to do to survive," he continues, but he's made his point, and Rachelle knows she crossed a line.

"I'm sorry." Her voice is soft, and her eyes dart between the two of us. She swallows hard before speaking. "Um, Cami, I think I should get going."

"Do you want me to give you a ride? It's really late."

I don't want her running the three miles back to her house this time of night. She shouldn't have been out running this late to begin with, but then again, she probably wouldn't have done it in the first place if I had called her. My sister runs when she's worried or stressed out over something.

"No, I can text Jeremy."

"Text him and stay until he gets here," Ben tells her, but it's more like a command. I wait for Rachelle to fire back, but she doesn't. "I'm going to go back to bed. I've got to leave earlier than I expected. Kins texted. Girls need me to pick them up in the morning and drop them off at the library."

I nod, noting the way he kisses my head softly this time and breathes in my scent. He lets go and turns to leave the room again, but Rachelle's voice stops him.

"Please don't hurt her," she tells him, crossing the room to stand in front of him. I can feel the seriousness pouring off my sister. "I can see you care about her, but I know my sister. She's already decided you're the one."

"If I had my way, I'd marry her tomorrow." My heart flutters hard in my chest. The confession rocks me hard. I watch as he gives my sister a nod and leaves us hens to it.

"Holy shit, did he just say he wanted to marry me?" I ask out loud to no one in particular.

"I better be your fucking MOH." Rachelle chuckles and throws an arm around my shoulder. "Word of sisterly advice… Watch your teeth."

Nine

When Ben walks into the library with his girls, my heart leaps into my chest. His all-male presence sends tingles throughout my body as the memories of our weekend together surface fresh in my mind. He finds me immediately, and the moment our eyes meet, I feel the earth shift under my feet.

It's magic.

My hands itch to touch him.

My lips yearn for his taste.

It takes everything in me to stay put and not approach them. His girls are with him, and we never officially put a label on what we are, so I wait for him to decide what happens. It's possible that he hasn't told them about us yet, which I can understand.

But then he moves in my direction.

His dark brown eyes pin me in place, telling me to stay put, and I do. I couldn't move even if my life depended on it. He tells me with his eyes what I need to prepare for.

The girls know.

My heart swells, because without words he's told me what I am to him. But if I'm honest with myself, I already knew. Ben isn't the kind of man who would speak about marriage unless he was serious, and after what he told my sister last night, he's made his intention pretty clear.

The three of them stop in front of me. Ben leans down to press a sweet kiss on my mouth, and the girls coo. They literally fucking *coo* at us.

"Oh, my gosh, you guys are so cute," Kinsley giggles.

"I told you it was only a matter of time." Katie bounces on the balls of her feet. They watch as Ben places an arm around me and pulls me in close to him. "You know what, you should come with us this weekend. Dad's taking us to the fair."

Ben looks down at me expectantly, waiting for my response to his daughter's legit invitation.

"Um, yes, I'd like that very much," I tell her, feeling instant acceptance into their and their father's life. I wasn't sure how'd they take the news about us, but this is more than I expected.

"Mom is going to freak out." Kinsley giggles again before sneaking a photo of Ben and me with her phone and typing furiously onto it.

Wait, what?

I look up at Ben, feeling a surge of unease, but he's quick to dash it away.

"Relax," he whispers only for my ears. "Veronica

and Bill have been happily married for almost two years, and as good parents, we're a team."

I nod, understanding immediately. He's a good man and a good father, and regardless of the reasons his marriage ended, he would stay neutral for the girls.

"Cami, can I work with you today?" Katie asks, and I nod. Even though the girls don't report to me for their internship, if I ask, they can be assigned to me at any time.

"I'll be in the stacks today, so it'll be a bit boring," I warn, but I have a feeling I could be scrubbing toilets and she'd still want to be with me.

"Kins, Katie, you girls need to go check in before you're late," Ben tells them, and they both step forward to hug him goodbye, then dart off to make their check-in time. The library internship is an easy job, but they're strict about being on time, and it could cost them their spot. Ben tightens his hold at my waist. "Alone at last."

"I didn't expect that," I say, turning to face him. My shift doesn't officially start for another fifteen minutes, but I came early hoping to see him.

"Girls needed to know, especially with you moving in as soon as I can convince you of it." He smiles.

"Ben—" I start, but he stops me.

"It isn't too soon. This should have happened months ago when I first saw you, but I fucked up. The way I see it, you're mine, and I'm yours. Nothing and no one is going to change that." The seriousness of his words and the fact he's obviously given this some thought make me consider how real this has become for both of us. "You know how I feel, Cami, and since you didn't run for the hills after I told your sister I'm going to marry you the moment you let me, you feel the same. So why wait?"

I drag in a breath, mulling over his words.

What was supposed to be a night of hot sex and good company has transformed into a future filled with possibility with a man I've been in love with since the moment I saw him.

I've spent my entire life waiting for fate to give me the happily-ever-after I've only read in a book, and I'm not about to let it go.

"Yes," I laugh, lifting up onto my toes to press my lips against his, using the one line I've spent my life waiting to use. "A thousand times, yes."

Epilogue

CAMI

Katie beams down at us as she prepares to walk across the stage to accept her high school diploma. Her excitement is evident as she bounces on the balls of her feet, all but dancing.

Ben chuckles at the sight while holding on to our second son, Dylan. His toddler arms flail, nearly missing Ben's face. He's excited to see his big sister after watching the crowds of people surrounding us.

Ryan, our oldest son, sits quietly beside me, waiting for his sister to walk across the stage. Despite his calm and quiet demeanor, he'll be the one to cheer the loudest.

Kinsley stands beside her father. Now in her second year at the University of Berkley, she flew home for the week to be here for her sister and the birth of our third son, Tyler, who was due three days ago but is being stingy.

"Katie Grace Thompson," the principal's loud, booming voice announces her name finally. I stand, shouting with joy, when I feel a splash of warm liquid hit my feet.

Shit.

I look down in shock and feel Ben's gaze on me, my sudden silence alerting him.

Shit.

My water just broke.

Shit.

Looking up at him, I take a calming breath, ignoring the pain of my first official contraction.

"It's time," I say softly, gathering everyone's attention at once. A beat later, Ben passes Dylan to Kinsley and looks over his shoulder to where Katie is now standing bright eyed at the short metal gate separating the graduates from the crowd.

"I knew he was going to be born today!" she shouts, hopping over the barrier with her diploma in hand, waving off one of the teachers trying to stop her. "My baby brother's coming."

My heart nearly explodes from my chest when I realize she's made her way to my side and is holding Ryan's hand.

I feel a sudden surge of strength as my boys, my girls, and the most perfect man in the world push through the crowd, ready to welcome one more into our amazing family.

And it all started with the sweetest slow burn one night in Chicago.

THE END

Acknowledgments

Thank you to my family and friends for all their love and support.

To the Meat Market girls, thank you for taking a chance on a small-time author and letting me put my name next to yours! #yourfangirlforever

To you, the reader, for kicking ass and reading my words.

If enjoyed Ben and Cami, please feel free to leave a review!

<u>Copper Creek Series</u>

Skinny Dip

Gray and Aiden's Stories - COMING SOON

<u>The Lost Series</u>

Lost in Silence

Lost Without You

Lost in the Shadows

Lost in His Kiss

<u>The All Heart Series</u>

Donut Swipe Right

Slow Burn

HEARTfire

<u>Holiday and Heart</u>

His Christmas Miracles

<u>Fated Destiny Duet</u>

Spellbound

Irish Whiskey

<u>Rogue Enforcers</u>

Alarik

Roman - COMING 2022

<u>Standalones</u>

One Last Wish

Dare You

Mr. Somebody

Finding Hope

About Tracie Douglas

Surviving on caffeine most days, Tracie Douglas lives with her husband, two children, one dog, two cats and nine chickens. She spends her days chasing children and the fur baby, all while maintaining the illusion of sanity.

Her nights are spent toiling away at the keyboard, creating a world filled with hot men and strong women. She loves to read and write all types of books but tends to lean on the darker side of the spectrum. She's pretty handy with a crochet hook, too.

Tracie loves to hear from her readers!

Email: traciedouglas.author@gmail.com

9 798822 319927